THE
Fabulous
FRIEND
MACHINE

For WING DING,
THE CHICKEN WHO SURVIVED

Scholastic Canada Ltd.
604 King Street West, Toronto, Ontario M5V 1E1, Canada

Scholastic Inc.
557 Broadway, New York, NY 10012, USA

Scholastic Australia Pty Limited
PO Box 579, Gosford, NSW 2250, Australia

Scholastic New Zealand Limited
Private Bag 94407, Botany, Manukau 2163, New Zealand

Scholastic Children's Books
Euston House, 24 Eversholt Street, London NW1 1DB, UK

www.scholastic.ca

Library and Archives Canada Cataloguing in Publication
Bland, Nick, 1973-, author, illustrator
        The fabulous friend machine / written and illustrated by Nick Bland.
Originally published: Australia: Scholastic Australia, 2016.
ISBN 978-1-4431-5747-6 (hardback).--ISBN 978-1-4431-5748-3 (paperback)
        I. Title.
PZ7.B557Fa 2017   j823'.92   C2016-904600-1

6 5 4 3 2 1   Printed in China 38   17 18 19 20 21

THE Fabulous FRIEND Machine

NICK BLAND

Scholastic Canada Ltd.
Toronto New York London Auckland Sydney
Mexico City New Delhi Hong Kong Buenos Aires

Popcorn was, quite simply, the friendliest chicken at **FIDDLESTICKS FARM**. She insisted on saying *hello* to every animal every morning.

She used words like **wonderful**, **fabulous**, **splendid** and **fine** . . .

and brightened
everyone's day.

She was *wonderfully* kind . . . and *fabulously* helpful.

And she told the most *splendid* stories at milking time.

Popcorn was so friendly, she even won a prize for being the *friendliest* chicken at the **FARMYARD FAIR** three years in a row.

And every year, she gave her medal to someone who **_needed it more_**.
Popcorn was, quite simply, the friendliest chicken at **FIDDLESTICKS FARM**.

One morning, while Popcorn was visiting the horse, she was **dazzled** by a light in the corner.

It was coming from a *tiny* little screen. And on the tiny screen was an even *tinier* envelope.

Popcorn tapped the envelope and a word popped up. HELLO! it said.

How wonderfully friendly! she thought. She sent a message back.

HELLO!

Then another message arrived.
Then another . . . and another . . . and another.

Splendid! she thought.

It's a fabulous friend machine.

Popcorn went to morning tea with her friends as usual. But she was so busy sending messages, she didn't even look up to say *hello*.

The cows found her no fun at all  at milking time.

And she almost got *run over* crossing the road.

The more messages Popcorn sent, the more she received.

All day . . .

And all night.

The next morning, Popcorn decided she
wanted to meet her *fabulous* new friends.

She invited them all to a party . . . and completely forgot to invite her old friends.

She made a great big **double-fudge chocolate cake** and waited.

But when Popcorn's new friends arrived,
they weren't fabulous at all.

THEY WERE
WOLVES!

And they *didn't* want to eat
double-fudge chocolate cake.

THEY WANTED TO EAT . . .

Lucky for Popcorn, her fabulous old friends came up with a **brilliant** plan to save her.

And they arrived
just in time.

"GRRRR!"

The wolves ran back to the forest and they took the **FRIEND MACHINE** with them.

Popcorn thanked her friends and the *not-so-fabulous* friend machine was never spoken of again at **FIDDLESTICKS FARM...**